WHO'S WHO at the ZOO!

Written by Janet Palazzo-Craig
Illustrated by Ray Burns

Troll Associates

Library of Congress Cataloging in Publication Data

Palazzo-Craig, Janet.
  Who's who at the zoo!

  Summary: There are lots of animals at the zoo to see,
but the best of them all is a young chimpanzee.
  [1. Zoo animals—Fiction. 2. Stories in rhyme]
I. Burns, Raymond, 1924-   ill.   II. Title.
PZ8.3.P1564Wh   1986   [E]   85-14123
ISBN 0-8167-0658-1 (lib. bdg.)
ISBN 0-8167-0659-X (pbk.)

WHO'S WHO at the ZOO!

This morning is special—
I'm wide awake!
But why is it special,
for goodness' sake?

The birds are singing a pretty song.
The sun is shining—so come along!

I'll wake up Susie and Billy, too.
Today is the day we go to the zoo.

Hurry, eat breakfast.
Don't be late!
Let's get going—I just can't wait.

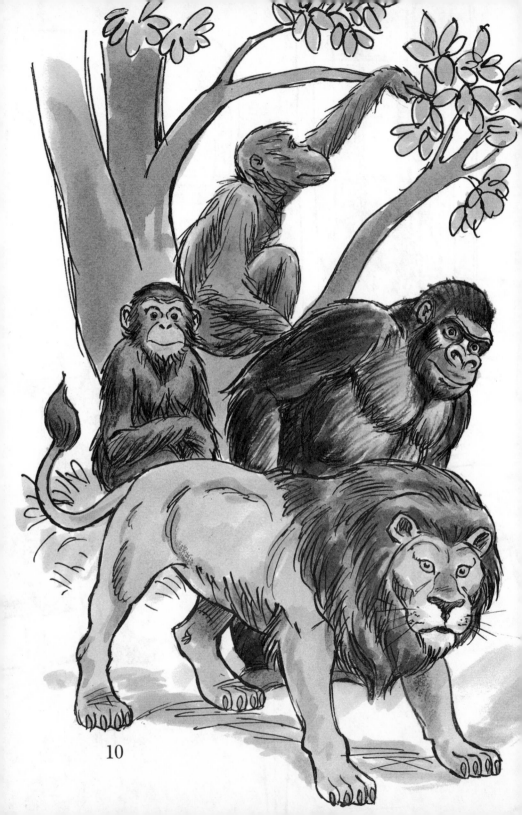

Today is the day for lions and
    monkeys,
for apes and orangutans,
tigers and donkeys.

Maybe we'll see a giraffe so tall,
or scurrying by, a mouse so small.

I see the sign.
It's high in the air.
I know what it means—
we're finally there!

In through the gate we go,
    one by one,
into the zoo to have lots of fun.

Look everybody, look what I see—
a big-eyed owl staring back at me!

What's that over there?
It's a zebra named Lizzie.
When she runs back and forth,
her stripes make you dizzy.

Animals here. Animals there.
Animals, animals—everywhere!
High in the trees
and low to the ground,
I see and hear animals,
making animal sounds.

18

Grunting and groaning,
muddy and big—
what can it be?
It must be a pig!

Here's Lenny the lion.
He lets out a roar.
Let's get away quick,
before he roars more.

Up stretches the elephant's trunk
like a tower.
She's filled it with water
and she gives us a shower.

A monkey is chattering high in a
tree,
swinging and screeching and
calling with glee.

This giant tortoise moves so very slow.
Let's hitch a ride and see where it might go.

Camels from deserts,
fish from the sea,
deer from the plains,
are all around me.

Bears from the woods
and birds in the air!
Animals, animals—everywhere!

What's in here?
What can it be?
I don't see a thing.
This cage is *empty*.

28

Can it be so? Can it really be true?
Have we seen every animal that
lives in the zoo?

I'm very tired. Let's take a rest.
Or let's get an ice-cream cone.
That would be best.

Susie likes strawberry.
Billy likes lime.
I like them all—
but that doesn't rhyme.

Eating our ice cream
under the tree,
here we are—
Susie, Billy, and me.

Suddenly, suddenly, up in the
tree—
I *think* I feel somebody looking
at me.

Eyes big and round,
who can it be?
Why, it's a baby—
a small chimpanzee.

Looking at us and giving a moan,
down jumps the chimp
and grabs Susie's cone.

Oh, what a chase!
Circling and jumping,
swinging and bumping!
There he goes around the
    bend.
Don't go away, chimp!
Come be our friend.

We've seen lots of animals.
We've seen the rest.
But of them all,
we think you're the best.

Here comes the zoo keeper.
She calls to the chimp,
"So there you are, you little imp.

"I've looked for you everywhere,
in corners and cracks,
in closets and crannies,
in cages and sacks.

"Thanks for helping me find Hank
　　the runaway.
His favorite trick is to hide once
　　a day.

"It's time to get back to your home,
little guy.
You've had an adventure.
But, first, say goodbye."

It's getting late.
We'd better go, too.
What a day,
such a day,
we've had at the zoo!